World of Reading

LEVEL 1

THIS IS BLACK WIDOW

Written by Clarissa Wong

Illustrated by Andrea Di Vito and Peter Pantazis

Based on the Marvel comic book series The Avengers

ABDO
Spotlight

MARVEL

Los Angeles
New York

Reader

ABDOPUBLISHING.COM

Reinforced library bound edition published in 2018 by Spotlight, a division of ABDO, PO Box 398166, Minneapolis, Minnesota 55439. Spotlight produces high-quality reinforced library bound editions for schools and libraries. Published by Marvel Press, an imprint of Disney Book Group.

Printed in the United States of America, North Mankato, Minnesota.
042017
092017

marvelkids.com
© 2015 MARVEL

THIS BOOK CONTAINS
RECYCLED MATERIALS

PUBLISHER'S CATALOGING-IN-PUBLICATION DATA

Names: Wong, Clarissa, author. | Di Vito, Andrea ; Pantazis, Peter, illustrators.
Title: Black Widow: this is Black Widow / writer: Clarissa Wong ; art: Andrea Di Vito ; Peter Pantazis.
Other titles: This is Black Widow
Description: Reinforced library bound edition. | Minneapolis, Minnesota : Spotlight, 2018. | Series: World of reading level 1
Summary: Go on an adventure with Marvel's expert spy and S.H.I.E.L.D. agent, Natasha Romanoff, otherwise known as Black Widow.
Identifiers: LCCN 2017936169 | ISBN 9781532140501 (lib. bdg.)
Subjects: LCSH: Avengers (Fictitious characters)--Juvenile fiction. | Superheroes--Juvenile fiction. | Adventure and adventurers--Juvenile fiction. | Comic books, strips, etc.--Juvenile fiction. | Graphic novels--Juvenile fiction.
Classification: DDC [Fic]--dc23
LC record available at https://lccn.loc.gov/2017936169

Spotlight
A Division of ABDO
abdopublishing.com

This is Natasha.

She is a secret agent.

She is also a spy.

She works for S.H.I.E.L.D.

She was an orphan.
She lived at the Red Room.

The Red Room was a secret camp.
It was an evil place.

The camp leaders trained
her to be a spy.
They taught her to steal.
She knew the Red Room was bad.

The Red Room was hurting people.
Natasha wanted to help people.
She wanted to fight for good.

She decided to join S.H.I.E.L.D. At first Nick Fury was unsure about her.

He knew she was good at spying.
Was she spying on him?
He wanted to make sure
she was telling the truth.

She helped the Avengers
stop the Red Room.
She led the Avengers
to the bad people.

Then Nick Fury could
trust Natasha.
He let her join S.H.I.E.L.D.
Her code name was Black Widow.

She wears black so no one notices her.
Black is also her favorite color.

Tony Stark gave her a weapon.
It is called the Widow's Bite.
It looks like bracelets.
But it is much more.

Watch out!
They shoot blasts.

Black Widow is quiet.

Black Widow is quick.

Black Widow is a good fighter.
She doesn't need Tony's help.
She can fight off aliens by herself!

She can flip in the air
and land on her feet.

She can kick high.

She can throw a good punch, too.
Look out!
She is prepared for anything.

She is good at hiding.

She can blend in with the crowd.

Can you find her?

She has red hair.

She is clever.
She can outsmart villains—no
matter how much bigger they are!

Just watch.
Black Widow kicks butt!

Black Widow can sneak into
any building.
She knows how to get in and out.
Nobody notices her.

She finds clues for S.H.I.E.L.D. The clues help S.H.I.E.L.D. solve many cases.

She helps the Avengers, too.
She is part of the team.

Natasha is good friends
with Hawkeye.
They are partners.
They work well together.

Black Widow is not always spying.
She practices ballet.
She is a graceful dancer.

Her ballet moves
help her in combat.
She can move with ease.

When she falls,
she picks herself up.

She never gives up.

She is the best at what she does.
She is Black Widow!